W9-DIY-592

Published by Creative Education, Inc.
123 S. Broad Street, Mankato, Minnesota 56001

Designed by Rita Marshall
Cover Illustration by Etienne Delessert

Copyright © 1990 Creative Education, Inc.
International copyrights reserved in all countries.
No part of this book may be reproduced in any form
without written permission from the publisher.
Printed in the United States of America.

Acknowledgment: Reprinted by permission of
Doubleday and Company, Inc.

Library of Congress Cataloging-in-Publication Data

Balzac, Honoré de, 1799–1850.
[Grande Bretèche. English]
La Grande Bretêche/by Honoré de Balzac: [translated by Clara Bell].
p. cm.
Summary: Curious about a neglected country estate which he has been asked to administer, a lawyer uncovers the story of a hideous revenge exacted by the former master at the expense of his unfaithful wife and her lover.
ISBN 0-88682-306-4
[1. Horror stories.] I. Title.
PZ7.B2144Gr 1989
[Fic]—dc20 89-37301
CIP
AC

LA GRANDE BRETÊCHE

HONORÉ DE BALZAC

CREATIVE EDUCATION INC.

"AH! MADAME," REPLIED THE DOCTOR, "I HAVE SOME APPALLING STORIES IN MY *collection. But each one has its proper hour in a conversation—you know the pretty jest recorded by Chamfort, and said to the Duc de Fronsac: 'Between your sally and the present moment lie ten bottles of champagne.' "*

"But it is two in the morning, and the story of Rosina has prepared us," said the mistress of the house.

"Tell us, Monsieur Bianchon!" was the cry on every side.

The obliging doctor bowed, and silence reigned.

"At about a hundred paces from Vendôme, on the banks of the Loire," said he, "stands an old brown house crowned with very high roofs, and so completely isolated that there is nothing near it, not even a fetid tannery or a squalid tavern, such as are commonly seen outside small towns. In front of this house is a garden down to the river, where the box shrubs, formerly clipped close to edge the walks, now straggle at their own will. A few willows, rooted in the stream, have grown up quickly like an enclosing fence, and half hide the house. The wild plants we call weeds have clothed the bank with their beautiful luxuriance. The fruit-trees, neglected for these ten years past, no longer bear a crop, and their suckers have formed a thicket. The espaliers are like a copse. The paths, once gravelled, are overgrown with purslane; but, to be accurate, there is no trace of a path.

"Looking down from the hill-top, to which cling the ruins of the old castle of the Dukes of Vendôme, the only spot whence the eye can see into this enclosure, we think that at a time, difficult now to determine, this spot of earth must have been the joy of some country gentleman devoted to roses and tulips, in a word, to horticulture, but above all a lover of choice fruit. An arbour is visible, or rather the wreck of an arbour, and under it a table still stands not entirely destroyed by time. At the aspect of this garden that is no more, the negative joys of the peaceful life of the provinces may be divined as we divine the history of a worthy tradesman when we read the epitaph on his tomb. To complete the mournful and tender impressions which seize the soul, on one of the walls there is a sundial graced with his homely Christian motto, *'Ultimam cogita.'*

"The roof of this house is dreadfully dilapidated; the outside shutters are always closed; the balconies are hung with swallows' nests; the doors are for ever shut. Straggling grasses have outlined the flagstones of the steps with green; the ironwork is rusty. Moon and sun, winter, summer, and snow have eaten into the wood, warped the boards, peeled off the paint. The dreary silence is broken only by birds and cats, pole-cats, rats, and mice, free to scamper round, and fight, and eat each other. An invisible hand has written over it all: 'Mystery.'

"If, prompted by curiosity, you go to look at this house from the street, you will see a large gate, with a round-arched top; the children have made many holes in it. I learned later that this door had been blocked for ten years. Through these irregular breaches you will see that the side towards the courtyard is in perfect harmony with the side towards the garden. The same ruin prevails. Tufts of weeds outline the paving stones; the walls are scored by enormous cracks, and the blackened coping is laced with a thousand festoons of pellitory. The stone steps are disjointed; the bell-cord is rotten; the gutter-spouts broken. What fire from heaven can have fallen there? By what decree has salt been sown on this dwelling? Has God been mocked here? Or was France betrayed? These are the questions we ask ourselves. Reptiles crawl over it, but give no reply. This empty and deserted house is a vast enigma of which the answer is known to none.

"It was formerly a little domain, held in fief, and is known as La Grande Bretêche. During my stay at Vendôme, where Despleins had left me in charge of a rich patient, the sight of this strange dwelling became one of my keenest pleasures. Was it not far better than a ruin? Certain memories of indisputable authenticity attach themselves to a ruin; but this house, still standing, though being slowly destroyed by an avenging hand, contained a secret, an unrevealed thought. At the very least it testified to a caprice. More than once in the evening I attacked the hedge, run wild, which surrounded the enclosure. I braved scratches, I got into this ownerless garden, this plot which was no longer public or private; I lingered there for hours gazing at the disorder. I would not, as the price of the story to which this strange scene no doubt was due, have asked a single question of any gossiping native. On that spot I wove delightful romances, and abandoned myself to little debauches of melancholy which enchanted me. If I had known the reason—perhaps quite commonplace—of this neglect, I should have lost the unwritten poetry which intoxicated me. To me this refuge represented the most various phases of human life, shadowed by misfortune; sometimes the calm of a cloister without the monks; sometimes the peace of the graveyard without the dead, who speak in the language of epitaphs; one day I saw in it the home of lepers; another, the house of the Atridae; but above all, I found there provincial life, with its contemplative ideas, its hour-glass existence. I often wept there, I never laughed.

"More than once I felt involuntary terrors as I heard overhead the dull hum of the wings of some hurrying wood-pigeon. The earth is dank; you must be on the watch for lizards, vipers, and frogs, wandering about with the wild freedom of nature; above all, you must have no fear of cold, for in a few minutes you feel an icy cloak settle on your shoulders, like the Commendatore's hand on Don Giovanni's neck.

"One evening I felt a shudder; the wind had turned an old rusty weathercock, and the creaking sounded like a cry from the house, at the very moment when I was finishing a gloomy drama to account for this monumental embodiment of woe. I returned to my inn, lost in gloomy thoughts. When I had supped, the hostess came in to my room with an air of mystery, and said, 'Monsieur, here is Monsieur Regnault."

" 'Who is Monsieur Regnault?'

" 'What, sir, do not you know Monsieur Regnault?—Well, that's odd,' said she, leaving the room.

"On a sudden I saw a man appear, tall, slim, dressed in black, hat in hand, who came in like a ram ready to butt his opponent, showing a receding forehead, a small pointed head, and a colourless face of the hue of a glass of dirty water. You would have taken him for an usher. The stranger wore an old coat, much worn at the seams; but he had a diamond in his shirt frill, and gold rings in his ears.

" 'Monsieur,' said I, 'whom have I the honour of addressing?'—He took a chair, placed himself in front of my fire, put his hat on my table, and answered while he rubbed his hands: 'Dear me, it is very cold.—Monsieur, I am Monsieur Regnault."

"I was encouraging myself by saying to myself, *'Il bondo cani!*

Seek!'

" 'I am,' he went on, 'notary at Vendôme.'

" 'I am delighted to hear it, Monsieur,' I exclaimed. 'But I am not in a position to make a will for reasons best known to myself.'

" 'One moment!' said he, holding up his hand as though to gain silence. "Allow me, Monsieur, allow me! I am informed that you sometimes go to walk in the garden of La Grande Bretêche.'

" 'Yes, Monsieur.'

" 'One moment!' said he, repeating his gesture. 'That constitutes a misdemeanour. Monsieur, as executor under the will of the late Comtesse de Merret, I come in her name to beg you to discontinue the practice. One moment! I am not a Turk, and do not wish to make a crime of it. And besides, you are free to be ignorant of the circumstances which compel me to leave the finest mansion in Vendôme to fall into ruin. Nevertheless, Monsieur, you must be a man of education, and you should know that the laws forbid, under heavy penalties, any trespass on enclosed property. A hedge is the same as a wall. But, the state in which the place is left may be an excuse for your curiosity. For my part, I should be quite content to make you free to come and go in the house; but being bound to respect the will of the testatrix, I have the honour, Monsieur, to beg that you will go into the garden no more. I myself, Monsieur, since the will was read, have never set foot in the house, which, as I had the honour of informing you, is part of the estate of the late Madame de

Merret. We have done nothing there but verify the number of doors and windows to assess the taxes I have to pay annually out of the funds left for that purpose by the late Madame de Merret. Ah! my dear sir, her will made a great commotion in the town.'

"The good man paused to blow his nose. I respected his volubility, perfectly understanding that the administration of Madame de Merret's estate had been the most important event of his life, his reputation, his glory, his Restoration. As I was forced to bid farewell to my beautiful reveries and romances, I was to reject learning the truth on official authority.

" 'Monsieur,' said I, 'would it be indiscreet if I were to ask you the reasons for such eccentricity?'

"At these words an expression, which revealed all the pleasure which men feel who are accustomed to ride a hobby, overspread the lawyer's countenance. He pulled up the collar of his shirt with an air, took out his snuff-box, opened it, and offered me a pinch; on my refusing, he took a large one. He was happy! A man who has no hobby does not know all the good to be got out of life. A hobby is the happy medium between a passion and a monomania. At this moment I understood the whole bearing of Sterne's charming passion, and had a perfect idea of the delight with which my uncle Toby, encouraged by Trim, bestrode his hobby-horse.

" 'Monsieur,' said Monsieur Regnault, 'I was head clerk in Monsieur Roguin's office, in Paris. A first-rate house, which you may have heard mentioned? No! An unfortunate bankruptcy made it famous.—Not having money enough to purchase a practice in Paris at the price to which they were run up in 1816, I came here and bought my predecessor's business. I had relations in Vendôme; among others, a wealthy aunt, who allowed me to marry her daughter. —Monsieur,' he went on after a little pause, 'three months after being licensed by the Keeper of the Seals, one evening, as I was going to bed—it was before my marriage—I was sent for by Madame la Comtesse de Merret, to her

Château of Merret. Her maid, a good girl, who is now a servant in this inn, was waiting at my door with the Countess's own carriage. Ah! one moment! I ought to tell you that Monsieur le Comte de Merret had gone to Paris to die two months before I came here. He came to a miserable end, flinging himself into every kind of dissipation. You understand?

" 'On the day when he left, Madame la Comtesse had quitted La Grande Bretêche, having dismantled it. Some people even say that she had burnt all the furniture, the hangings—in short, all the chattels and furniture whatever used in furnishing the premises now let by the said M.—(Dear! What am I saying? I beg your pardon, I thought I was dictating a lease.)—In short, that she burnt everything in the meadow at Merret. Have you been to Merret, Monsieur?—No,' said he, answering himself. 'Ah, it is a very fine place.'

" 'For about three months previously,' he went on, with a jerk of his head, 'the Count and

Countess had lived in a very eccentric way; they admitted no visitors; Madame lived on the ground floor, and Monsieur on the first floor. When the Countess was left alone she was never seen excepting at church. Subsequently, at home, at the château, she refused to see the friends, whether gentlemen or ladies, who went to call on her. She was already very much altered when she left La Grande Bretêche to go to Merret. That dear lady—I say dear lady, for it was she who gave me this diamond, but indeed I saw her but once—that kind lady was very ill; she had, no doubt, given up all hope, for she died without choosing to send for a doctor; indeed, many of our ladies fancied she was not quite right in her head. Well, sir, my curiosity was strangely excited by hearing that Madame de Merret had need of my services. Nor was I the only person who took an interest in the affair. That very night, though it was already late, all the town knew that I was going to Merret.

" 'The waiting-woman replied but vaguely to the questions I asked her on the way; nevertheless, she told me that her mistress had received the Sacrament in the course of the day at the hands of the Curé of Merret, and seemed unlikely to live through the night. It was about eleven when I reached the château. I went up the great staircase. After crossing some large, lofty, dark rooms, diabolically cold and damp, I reached the state bedroom where the Countess lay. From the rumours that were current concerning this lady (Monsieur, I should never end if I were to repeat all the tales that were told about her), I had imagined her a coquette. Imagine, then, that I had great difficulty in seeing her in the great bed where she was lying. To be sure, to light this enormous room, with old-fashioned heavy cornices, and so thick with dust that merely to see it was enough to make you sneeze, she had only an old Argand lamp. Ah! but you have not been to Merret. Well, the bed is one of those old-world beds, with the high tester hung with flowered chintz. A small table stood by the bed, on which I saw an "Imitation of Christ," which, by the way, I bought for my wife, as well as the lamp. There were also a deep armchair for her confidential maid, and two small chairs. There was no fire. That was all the furniture; not enough to fill ten lines in an inventory.

" 'My dear sir, if you had seen, as I then saw, that vast room, papered and hung with brown, you would have felt yourself transported into a scene of romance. It was icy, nay more, funereal,' and he lifted his hand with a theatrical gesture and paused.

" 'By dint of seeking, as I approached the bed, at last I saw Madame de Merret, under the glimmer of the lamp, which fell on the pillows. Her face was as yellow as wax, and as narrow as two folded hands. The Countess had a lace cap showing abundant hair, but as white as linen thread. She was sitting up in bed, and seemed to keep upright with great difficulty. Her large black eyes, dimmed by fever, no doubt, and half-dead already, hardly moved under the bony arch of her eyebrows.—There,' he added, pointing to his own brow. 'Her forehead was clammy; her fleshless hands were like bones covered with soft skin; the veins and muscles were perfectly visible. She must have been very handsome; but at this moment I was startled into an indescribable emotion at the sight. Never, said those who wrapped her in her shroud, had any living creature been so emaciated and lived. In short, it was awful to behold! Sickness had so consumed that woman, that she was no more than a phantom. Her lips, which were pale violet, seemed to me not to move when she spoke to me.

" 'Though my profession has familiarized me with such spectacles, by calling me not unfrequently to the bedside of the dying to record their last wishes, I confess that families in tears and the agonies I have seen were as nothing in comparison to this lonely and silent woman in her vast château. I heard not the least sound, I did not perceive the movement which the sufferer's breathing ought to have given to the sheets that covered her, and I stood motionless, absorbed in looking at her in a sort of stupor. In fancy I am there still.—At last her large eyes moved; she tried to raise her right hand, but it fell back on the bed, and she uttered these words, which came like a breath, for her voice was no longer a voice: "I have waited for you with the greatest impatience." A bright flush rose to her cheeks. It was a great effort to her to speak.

" 'Madame," I began. She signed to me to be silent. At that moment the old housekeeper rose and said in my ear, "Do not speak; Madame la Comtesse is not in a state to bear the slightest noise, and what you would say might agitate her."

" 'I sat down. A few instants after, Madame de Merret collected all her remaining strength to move her right hand, and slipped it, not without infinite difficulty, under the bolster; she then paused a moment. With a last effort she withdrew her hand; and when she brought out a sealed paper, drops of perspiration rolled from her brow. "I place my will in your hands —Oh! God! Oh!" and that was all. She clutched a crucifix that lay on the bed, lifted it hastily to her lips, and died.

" 'The expression of her eyes still makes me shudder as I think of it. She must have suffered much! There was joy in her last glance, and it remained stamped on her dead eyes.

" 'I brought away the will, and when it was opened I found that Madame de Merret had appointed me her executor. She left the whole of her property to the hospital of Vendôme excepting a few legacies. But these were her instructions as relating to La Grande Bretêche: She ordered me to leave the place, for fifty years counting from the day of her death, in the state in which it might be at the time of her decease, forbidding anyone, whoever he might be, to enter the apartments, prohibiting any repairs whatever, and even settling a salary to pay watchmen if it were needful to secure the absolute fulfilment of her intentions. At the expiration of that term, if the will of the testatrix has been duly carried out, the house is to become the property of my heirs, for, as you know, a notary cannot take a bequest. Otherwise La

Grande Bretêche reverts to the heirs-at-law, but on condition of fulfilling certain conditions set forth in a codicil to the will, which is not to be opened till the expiration of the said term of fifty years. The will has not been disputed, so——' And without finishing his sentence, the lanky notary looked at me and with an air of triumph; I made him quite happy by offering him my congratulations.

" 'Monsieur,' I said in conclusion, 'you have so vividly impressed me that I fancy I see the dying woman whiter than her sheets; her glittering eyes frighten me; I shall dream of her tonight.—But you must have formed some idea as to the instructions contained in that extraordinary will.'

" 'Monsieur,' said he, with comical reticence, 'I never allow myself to criticize the conduct of a person who honours me with the gift of a diamond.'

"However, I soon loosened the tongue of the discreet notary of Vendôme, who communicated to me, not without long digressions, the opinions of the deep politicians of both sexes whose judgments are law in Vendôme. But these opinions were so contradictory, so diffuse, that I was near falling asleep in spite of the interest I felt in this authentic history. The notary's ponderous voice and monotonous accent, accustomed no doubt to listen to himself and to make himself listened to by his clients or fellow-townsmen, were too much for my curiosity. Happily, he soon went away.

" 'Ah, ha, Monsieur,' said he on the stairs, 'a good many persons would be glad to live five-and-forty years longer; but—one moment!' and he laid the first finger of his right hand to his nostril with a cunning look, as much as to say, 'Mark my words!—To last as long as that—as long as that,' said he, 'you must not be past sixty now.'

"I closed my door, having been roused from my apathy by this last speech, which the notary thought very funny; then I sat down in my arm-chair with my feet on the fire-dogs. I had lost myself in a romance *à la* Radcliffe, constructed on the juridical base given me by Monsieur Regnault, when the door, opened by a woman's cautious hand, turned on the hinges. I saw my landlady come in, a buxom, florid dame, always good-humoured, who had missed her calling in life. She was a Fleming, who ought to have seen the light in a picture by Teniers.

" 'Well, Monsieur,' said she, 'Monsieur Regnault has no doubt been giving you his history of La Grande Bretêche?'

" 'Yes, Madame Lepas.'

" 'And what did he tell you?'

"I repeated in a few words the creepy and sinister story of Madame de Merret. At each sentence my hostess put her head forward, looking at me with an innkeeper's keen scrutiny, a happy compromise between the instinct of a police constable, the astuteness of a spy, and the cunning of a dealer.

" 'My good Madame Lepas,' said I as I ended, 'you seem to know more about it. Heh? If not, why have you come up to me?'

" 'On my word, as an honest woman—'

" 'Do not swear; your eyes are big with a secret. You knew Monsieur de Merret; what sort of man was he?'

" 'Monsieur de Merret—well, you see he was a man you never could see the top of, he was so tall! A very good gentleman, from Picardy, and who had, as we say, his head close to his cap. He paid for everything down, so as never to have difficulties with anyone. He was hot-tempered, you see! All our ladies liked him very much.'

" 'Because he was hot-tempered?' I asked her.

" 'Well, may be,' said she; 'and you may suppose, sir, that a man had to have something to show for a figure-head before he could marry Madame de Merret, who, without any reflection on others, was the handsomest and richest heiress in our parts. She had about twenty thousand francs a year. All the town was at the wedding; the bride was pretty and sweet-looking, quite a gem of a woman. Oh, they were a handsome couple in their day!'

" 'And were they happy together?"

" 'Hm, hm! so-so—so far as can be guessed, for, as you may suppose, we of the common sort were not hail-fellow-well-met with them.—Madame de Merret was a kind woman and very pleasant, who had no doubt sometimes to put up with her husband's tantrums. But though he was rather haughty, we were fond of him. After all, it was his place to behave so. When a man is a born nobleman, you see——'

" 'Still, there must have been some catastrophe for Monsieur and Madame de Merret to part so violently?"

" 'I did not say there was any catastrophe, sir. I know nothing about it.'

" 'Indeed. Well, now, I am sure you know everything.'

" 'Well, sir, I will tell you the whole story.—When I saw Monsieur Regnault go up to see you, it struck me that he would speak to you about Madame de Merret as having to do with La Grande Bretêche. That put it into my head to ask your advice, sir, seeming to me that you are a man of good judgment and incapable of playing a poor woman like me false—for I never did anyone a wrong, and yet I am tormented by my conscience. Up to now I have never dared to say a word to the people of these parts; they are all chattermags, with tongues like knives. And never till now, sir, have I had any traveller here who stayed so long in the inn as you have, and to whom I could tell the history of the fifteen thousand francs——'

" 'My dear Madame Lepas, if there is anything in your story of a nature to compromise me,' I said, interrupting the flow of her words, 'I would not hear it for all the world.'

" 'You need have no fears,' she said; 'you will see.'

"Her eagerness made me suspect that I was not the only person to whom my worthy landlady had communicated the secret of which I was to be sole possessor, but I listened.

" 'Monsieur,' said she, 'when the Emperor sent the Spaniards here, prisoners of war and others, I was required to lodge at the charge of the Government a young Spaniard sent to Vendôme on parole. Notwithstanding his parole, he had to show himself every day to the sub-prefect. He was a Spanish grandee—neither more nor less. He had a name in *os* and *dia,* something like Bagos de Férédia. I wrote his name down in my books, and you may see it if you like. Ah! he was a handsome young fellow for a Spaniard, who are all ugly they say. He was not more than five feet two or three in height, but so well made; and he had little hands that he kept so beautifully! Ah! you should have seen them. He had as many brushes for his hands as a woman has for her toilet. He had thick, black hair, a flame in his eye, a somewhat coppery complexion, but which I admired all the same. He wore the finest linen I have ever seen, though I have had princesses to lodge here, and, among others, General Bertrand, the Duc and Duchesse d'Abrantés, Monsieur Descazes, and the King of Spain. He did not eat much, but he had such polite and amiable ways that it was impossible to owe him a grudge for that. Oh! I was very fond of him, though he did not say four words to me in a day, and it was impossible to have the least bit of talk with him; if he was spoken to, he did not answer; it is a way, a mania they all have, it would seem.

" 'He read his breviary like a priest, and went to Mass and all the services quite regularly. And where did he post himself?—we found this out later.—Within two yards of Madame de Merret's chapel. As he took that place the very first time he entered the church, no one imagined that there was any purpose in it. Besides, he never raised his nose above his book, poor young man! And then, Monsieur, of an evening he went for a walk on the hill among the ruins of the old castle. It was his only amusement, poor man; it reminded him of his native land. They say that Spain is all hills!

" 'One evening, a few days after he was sent here, he was out very late. I was rather uneasy when he did not come in till just on the stroke of midnight; but we all got used to his whims; he took the key of the door, and we never sat up for him. He lived in a house belonging to us in the Rue des Casernes. Well, then, one of our stable-boys told us one evening that, going down to wash the horses in the river, he fancied he had seen the Spanish grande swimming some little way off, just like a fish. When he came in, he told him to be careful of the weeds, and he seemed put out at having been seen in the water.

" 'At last, Monsieur, one day, or rather one morning, we did not find him in his room; he had not come back. By hunting through his things, I found a written paper in the drawer of his table, with fifty pieces of Spanish gold of the kind they call doubloons, worth about five thousand francs; and in a little sealed box ten thousand francs' worth of diamonds. The paper said that in case he should not return, he left us his money and these diamonds in trust to found Masses to thank God for his escape and for his salvation.

" 'At that time I still had my husband, who ran off in search of him. And this is the queer part of the story: he brought back the Spaniard's clothes, which he had found under a big stone on a side of breakwater along the river bank, nearly opposite La Grande Bretĉhe. My husband went so early that no one saw him. After reading the letter, he burnt the clothes, and, in obedience to Count Féredia's wish, we announced that he had escaped.

" 'The sub-prefect set all the constabulary at his heels; I pshaw! he was never caught. Lepas believed that the Spaniard drowned himself. I, sir, have never thought so; I believe, on contrary, that he had something to do with the business about Madame de Merret, seeing that Rosalie told me that the crucifix her mistress was so fond of that she had it buried with her, made of ebony and silver; now in the early days of his stay here, Monsieur Férédia had one of ebony and silver which I never saw later.—And now, Monsieur, do not you say that I need have no remorse about the Spaniard's fifteen thousand francs? Are they really and truly mine?'

" 'Certainly.—But have you never tried to question Rosa.' said I.

" 'Oh, to be sure I have, sir. But what is to be done? That girl is like a wall. She knows something, but it is impossible to make her talk.'

"After chatting with me for a few minutes, my hostess left me a prey to vague and sinister thoughts, to romantic curiosity, and a religious dread, not unlike the deep emotion which comes upon us when we go into a dark church at night and discern a feeble light glimmering under a lofty vault—a dim figure glides across—the sweep of a gown or of a priest's cassock is audible—and we shiver! La Grande Bretêche, with its rank grasses, its shuttered windows, its rusty ironwork, its locked doors, its deserted rooms, suddenly rose before me in fantastic vividness. I tried to get into the mysterious dwelling to search out the heart of this solemn story, this drama which had killed three persons.

"Rosalie became in my eyes the most interesting being in Vendôme. As I studied her, I detected signs of an inmost thought, in spite of the blooming health that glowed in her dimpled face. There was in her soul some element of truth or of hope, her manner suggested a secret, like the expression of devout souls who pray in excess, or of a girl who has killed her child and for ever hears its last cry. Nevertheless, she was simple and clumsy in her ways; her vacant smile had nothing criminal in it, and you would have pronounced her innocent only from seeing the large red and blue checked kerchief that covered her stalwart bust, tucked into the tight-laced square bodice of a lilac-and-white-striped gown. 'No,' said I to myself, 'I will not quit Vendôme without knowing the whole history of La Grande Bretêche. To achieve this end, I will make love to Rosalie if it proves necessary.'

"Rosalie!' said I one evening.

" 'Your servant, sir?'

" 'You are not married?' She started a little.

" 'Oh! there is no lack of men if ever I take a fancy to be miserable!' she replied, laughing. She got over her agitation at once; for every woman, from the highest lady to the inn-servant inclusive, has a native presence of mind.

" 'Yes; you are fresh and good-looking enough never to lack lovers! But tell me, Rosalie, why did you become an inn-servant on leaving Madame de Merret? Did she not leave you some little annuity?'

" 'Oh yes, sir. But my place here is the best in all the town of Vendôme.'

"This reply was such a one as judges and attorneys call evasive. Rosalie, as it seemed to me, held in this romantic affair the place of a middle square of the chess board; she was at the very centre of the interest and of the truth; she appeared to me to be tied into the knot of it. It was not a case for ordinary love-making; this girl contained the last chapter of a romance, and from that moment all my attentions were devoted to Rosalie. By dint of studying the girl, I observed in her, as in every woman whom we make our ruling thought, a variety of good qualities; she was clean and neat; she was handsome, I need not say; she soon was possessed of every charm that desire can lend to a woman in whatever rank of life. A fort-night after the notary's visit, one evening, or rather one morning, in the small hours, I said to Rosalie:

" 'Come, tell me all you know about Madame de Merret.'

" 'Oh!' she cried in terror, 'do not ask me that, Monsieur Horace!'

"Her handsome features clouded over, her bright colouring grew pale, and her eyes lost their artless, liquid brightness.

" 'Well,' she said, 'I will tell you; but keep the secret carefully.'

" 'All right, my child; I will keep all your secrets with a thief's honour, which is the most loyal known.'

" 'If it is all the same to you,' said she, 'I would rather it should be with your own.'

"Thereupon she set her head-kerchief straight, and settled herself to tell the tale; for there is no doubt a particular attitude of confidence and security is necessary to the telling of a narrative. The best tales are told at a certain hour—just as we are all here at table. No one ever told a story well standing up, or fasting.

"If I were to reproduce exactly Rosalie's diffuse eloquence, a whole volume would scarcely contain it. Now, as the event of which she gave me a confused account stands exactly midway between the notary's gossip and that of Madame Lepas, as precisely as the middle term of a rule-of-three sum stands between the first and third, I have only to relate it in as few words as may be. I shall therefore be brief.

"The room at La Grande Bretêche in which Madame de Merret slept was on the ground floor; a little cupboard in the wall, about four feet deep, served her to hang her dresses in. Three months before the evening of which I have to relate the events, Madame de Merret had been seriously ailing, so much so that her husband had left her to herself, and had his own bedroom on the first floor. By one of those accidents which it is impossible to foresee, he came in that evening two hours later than usual from the club, where he went to read the papers and talk politics with the residents in the neighbourhood. His wife supposed him to have come in, to be in bed and asleep. But the invasion of

France had been the subject of a very animated discussion; the game of billiards had waxed vehement; he had lost forty francs, an enormous sum at Vendôme, where everybody is thrifty, and where social habits are restrained within the bounds of a simplicity worthy of all praise, and the foundation perhaps of a form of true happiness which no Parisian would care for.

"For some time past Monsieur de Merret had been satisfied to ask Rosalie whether his wife was in bed; on the girl's replying always in the affirmative, he at once went to his own room, with the good faith that comes of habit and confidence. But this evening, on coming in, he took it into his head to go to see Madame de Merret, to tell her of his ill-luck, and perhaps to find consolation. During dinner he had observed that his wife was very becomingly dressed; he reflected as he came home from the club that his wife was certainly much better, that convalescence had improved her beauty, discovering it, as husbands discover everything, a little too late. Instead of calling Rosalie, who was in the kitchen at the moment watching the cook and the coachman playing a puzzling hand at cards, Monsieur de Merret made his way to his wife's room by the light of his lantern, which he set down on the lowest step of the stairs. His step, easy to recognize, rang under the vaulted passage.

"At the instant when the gentleman turned the key to enter his wife's room, he fancied he heard the door shut of the closet of which I have spoken; but when he went in, Madame de Merret was alone, standing in front of the fire-place. The unsuspecting husband fancied that Rosalie was in the cupboard; nevertheless, a doubt, ringing in his ears like a peal of bells, put him on his guard; he looked at his wife, and read in her eyes an indescribably anxious and haunted expression.

" 'You are very late,'' said she.—Her voice, usually so clear and sweet, struck him as being slightly husky.

"Monsieur de Merret made no reply, for at this moment Rosalie came in. This was like a thunderclap. He walked up and down the room, going from one window to another at a regular pace, his arms folded.

" 'Have you had bad news, or are you ill?' his wife asked him timidly, while Rosalie helped her to undress. He made no reply.

" 'You can go, Rosalie,' said Madame de Merret to her maid; 'I can put in my curl-papers myself,'—She scented disaster at the mere aspect of her husband's face, and wished to be alone with him. As soon as Rosalie was gone, or supposed to be gone, for she lingered a few minutes in the passage, Monsieur de Merret came and stood facing his wife, and said coldly, 'Madame, there is someone in your cupboard!' She looked at her husband calmly, and replied quite simply, 'No, Monsieur.'

"This 'No' wrung Monsieur de Merret's heart; he did not believe it; and yet his wife had never appeared purer or more saintly than she seemed to be at this moment. He rose to go and open the closet door. Madame de Merret took his hand, stopped him, looked at him sadly, and said in a voice of strange emotion, 'Remember, if you should find no one there, everything must be at an end between you and me.'

"The extraordinary dignity of his wife's attitude filled him with deep esteem for her, and inspired him with one of those resolves which need only a grander stage to become immortal.

" 'No, Josephine,' he said, 'I will not open it. In either event we should be parted for ever. Listen; I know all the purity of your soul, I know you lead a saintly life, and would not commit a deadly sin to save your life.'—At these words Madame de Merret looked at her husband with a haggard stare—'See, here is your crucifix,' he went on. 'Swear to me before God that there is no one in there; I will believe you—I will never open that door.'

"Madame de Merret took up the crucifix and said, 'I swear it.'

" 'Louder,' said her husband; 'and repeat: "I swear before God that there is nobody in that closet." ' She repeated the words without flinching.

" 'That will do,' said Monsieur de Merret coldly. After a moment's silence: 'You have there a fine piece of work which I never saw before,' said he, examining the crucifix of ebony and silver, very artistically wrought.

" 'I found it at Duvivier's; last year when that troop of Spanish prisoners came through Vendôme, he bought it of a Spanish monk.'

" 'Indeed,' said Monsieur de Merret, hanging the crucifix on its nail; and he rang the bell.

"He had not to wait for Rosalie. Monsieur de Merret went forward quickly to meet her, led her into the bay of the window that looked on to the garden, and said to her in an undertone:

" 'I know that Gorenflot wants to marry you, that poverty alone prevents your setting up house, and that you told him you would not be his wife till he found means to become a master mason.—Well, go and fetch him; tell him to come here with his trowel and tools. Contrive to wake no one in his house but himself. His reward will be beyond your wishes. Above all, go out without saying a word—or else!' and he frowned.

"Rosalie was going, and he called her back. 'Here, take my latch-key,' said he.

" 'Jean!' Monsieur de Merret called in a voice of thunder down the passage. Jean, who was both coachman and confidential servant, left his cards and came.

" 'Go to bed, all of you,' said his master, beckoning him to come close; and the gentleman added in a whisper, 'When they are all asleep—mind, *asleep*—you understand?—come down and tell me.'

"Monsieur de Merret, who had never lost sight of his wife while giving his orders, quietly came back to her at the fireside, and began to tell her the details of the game of billiards and the discussion at the club. When Rosalie returned she found Monsieur and Madame de Merret conversing amiably.

"Not long before this Monsieur de Merret had had new ceilings made to all the reception-rooms on the ground floor. Plaster is very scarce at Vendôme; the price is enhanced by the cost of carriage; the gentleman had therefore had a considerable quantity delivered to him, knowing that he could always find purchasers for what might be left. It was this circumstance which suggested the plan he carried out.

" 'Gorenflot is here, sir,' said Rosalie in a whisper.

" 'Tell him to come in,' said her master aloud.

"Madame de Merret turned paler when she saw the mason.

" 'Gorenflot,' said her husband, 'go and fetch some bricks from the coach-house; bring enough to wall up the door of this cupboard; you can use the plaster that is left for cement.' Then, dragging Rosalie and the workman close to him—'Listen, Gorenflot,' said he, in a low voice, 'You are to sleep here to-night, but to-morrow morning you shall have a passport to take you abroad to a place I will tell you of. I will give you six thousand francs for your journey. You must live in that town for ten years; if you find you do not like it, you may settle in another, but it must be in the same country. Go through Paris and wait there till I join you. I will there give you an agreement for six thousand francs more, to be paid to you on your return, provided you have carried out the conditions of the bargain. For that price you are to keep perfect silence as to what you have to do this night. To you, Rosalie, I will secure ten thousand francs, which will not be paid to you till your wedding day, and on condition of your marrying Gorenflot; but, to get married, you must hold your tongue. If not, no wedding gift!'

" 'Rosalie,' said Madame de Merret, 'come and brush my hair.'

"Her husband quietly walked up and down the room, keeping an eye on the door, on the mason, and on his wife, but without any insulting display of suspicion. Gorenflot could not help making some noise. Madame de Merret seized a moment when he was unloading some bricks, and when her husband was at the other end of the room, to say to Rosalie: 'My dear child, I will give you a thousand francs a year if only you will tell Gorenflot to leave a crack at the bottom.' Then she added aloud quite cooly: 'You had better help him.'

"Monsieur and Madame de Merret were silent all the time while Gorenflot was walling up the door. This silence was intentional on the husband's part; he did not wish to give his wife the opportunity of saying anything with a double meaning. On Madame de Merret's side it was pride or prudence. When the wall was half built up the cunning mason took advantage of his master's back being turned to break one of the two panes in the top of the door with a blow of his pick. By this Madame de Merrit understood that Rosalie had spoken to Gorenflot. They all three then saw the face of a dark, gloomy-looking man, with black hair and flaming eyes.

"Before her husband turned round again the poor woman had nodded to the stranger, to whom the signal was meant to convey, 'Hope.'

"At four o'clock, as day was dawning, for it was the month of September, the work was done. The mason was placed in charge of Jean, and Monsieur de Merret slept in his wife's room.

"Next morning when he got up he said with apparent carelessness, 'Oh, by the way, I must go to the Mairie for the passport.' He put on his hat, took two or three steps towards the door, paused, and took the crucifix. His wife was trembling with joy.

" 'He will go to Duvivier's,' thought she.

"As soon as he had left, Madame de Merret rang for Rosalie, and then in a terrible voice she cried: 'The pick! Bring the pick! and set to work. I saw how Gorenflot did it yesterday; we shall have time to make a gap and build it up again.'

"In an instant Rosalie had brought her mistress a sort of cleaver; she, with a vehemence of which no words can give an idea, set to work to demolish the wall. She had already got out a few bricks, when, turning to deal a stronger blow than before, she saw behind her Monsieur de Merret. She fainted away.

" 'Lay Madame on her bed,' said he coldly.

"Foreseeing what would certainly happen in his absence, he had laid this trap for his wife;

he had merely written to the Mairie and sent for Duvivier. The jeweller arrived just as the disorder in the room had been repaired.

" 'Duvivier,' asked Monsieur de Merret, 'did not you buy some crucifixes of the Spaniards who passed through the town?'

" 'No, Monsieur.'

" 'Very good; thank you,' said he, flashing a tiger's glare at his wife. 'Jean,' he added, turning to his confidential valet, 'you can serve my meals here in Madame de Merret's room. She is ill, and I shall not leave her till she recovers.'

"The cruel man remained in his wife's room for twenty days. During the earlier time, when there was some little noise in the closet, and Josephine wanted to intercede for the dying man, he said, without allowing her to utter a word, 'You swore on the Cross that there was no one there.' "

After this story all the ladies rose from the table, and thus the spell under which Bianchon had held them was broken. But there were some among them who had almost shivered at the last words.